A Place Called
KINDERGARTEN

By JESSICA HARPER

pictures by
G. BRIAN KARAS

G. P. PUTNAM'S SONS

The animals in the barn were happy. The sun was rising over the oak tree and it was time for Tommy, the boy, to come down from the big house.

He came every day. He'd bring the horse an apple and rub his dappled nose. He'd feed the sheep a biscuit and scratch her woolly back.

He'd give the hen some corn and watch her sort
and peck at the kernels. He'd always have a fistful of
dandelions for the cow, which she considered a delicacy.

Sometimes Tommy would sing to them, a song about working on the railroad. And he'd throw his ball against the wall, over and over, which they found soothing. He always talked to them like humans, which made them feel important.

On this particular day, however,
Tommy did not appear at the usual time.

"Where can he be?" asked the horse.
"I can't imagine," said the sheep.
"He always comes," whined the hen.
"Where on earth is he?" wondered the cow.

(If you'd been there, listening in,
it would probably have sounded like this:
"NAY*Cluck***MOO***baa***NAY***Cluck***MOO***baa.*")

Just then the dog wandered by.
The barn animals didn't like the dog
much because he stole their food and
barked an awful lot, but he knew
what went on in the big house.

"Hey, where's Tommy today?" the cow asked the dog. "He usually comes when the sun rises over the oak tree."

"He's gone."

"Gone!" exclaimed the sheep.

"Yup, gone, in a big yellow bus."

"Well, where'd he go?" asked the horse, who was quite alarmed.

"I heard 'em talking." The dog yawned. "He went to a place called Kindergarten."

"Kindergarten! Where's that?" said the barn animals, almost all at once.

"Search me." The dog scratched an ear, and then loped off to see if the garbage can was tippy enough to be upended for a snack.

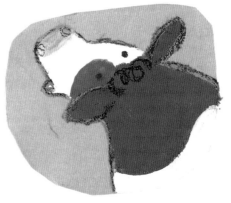

The animals burst into worried conversation.
"Where is Kindergarten?"
"What does it look like?"
"What will happen to Tommy there?"
"Will he ever come back?"

(If you'd been there, eavesdropping,
it would have sounded something like this:
"*Baabaabaabaa***MOOMOOMOOMOO**
*Cluckcluckcluckcluck***NAYNAYNAYNAY**...")

The sun had risen way past the oak
tree, and even past the barn, and still
Tommy did not come. The animals
were quiet, pretending to be calm.

The horse (who was the tallest) peeked out the window every two or three minutes. The cow patrolled the door. The sheep listened for boy-sized footsteps, and the hen paced in circles.

Finally, when the sun was
dropping toward the distant
cornfield, they heard him:

"Hall-OOOOOO! I'm HOME!!"

"YES!" bellowed the horse. And all the animals laughed and truly jumped for joy.

The hen even flew a little.

Into the barn
walked Tommy with the
biggest smile ever. His once-yellow
T-shirt looked like someone had
thrown a rainbow at it, splat!

"I've been to KINDERGARTEN!"
he announced.

"And I learned LOTS!"

The animals stood at polite and
smiling attention as Tommy explained.

"Listen to this!

A is for APPLE! That's for YOU!"

He handed the horse an apple and rubbed his nose like always. The horse smiled as much as you can when there's an apple in your mouth.

"B is for BISCUIT!

That's for you!"

He gave the sheep a biscuit and scratched her curly
wool till her eyes shut from the pleasure of it.

"C is for CORN!"

said Tommy.

He sprinkled the kernels at the feet of the hen
(if you can call them feet), who happily danced
and cackled and pecked.

He presented the cow with an extra-big handful.
She was DE-lighted!

"I learned all those letters today! And there's lots more to come. Tomorrow we start on E, then F and G and H (H is for HORSE, by the way) . . . and I finger-painted a picture of worms and we planted seeds and Mrs. Miller taught us about the world turning . . . hey, I learned a new song today! Wanna hear it?"

Without waiting for a response
from his animal audience,
who were all happily
chewing on things,
Tommy began:

"When Mother Nature
paints the sky,

She puts a rainbow in it.

Then she adds a
small, white cloud.

It only takes a minute."

Tommy sang his new song many times as
he threw the ball against the wall.

(If you'd been there, you'd have thought the animals
were singing along. It sounded sort of like this:

"Cluck BAAbaa MOOmoo NAY cluck BAA
cluck BAA moo NAYnay BAA cluck
BAAAA cluck moo NAY baa cluck MOO
cluck BAAAbaa MOO cluck NAYnay.")

When it was getting dark, Tommy was called
to the big house for supper. He yelled an extra-loud

„GuhNIGHT!!"

to the animals, threw the ball in the air as high
as it would go before he caught it and charged out toward the
house. For a long while, his song drifted down the hill to the barn.

The animals settled in. The horse nibbled hay
thoughtfully. The cow slurped some water and lay
down to sleep. The hen plopped cozily into her nest.

The sheep was not sleepy. "What do you suppose comes after H?" she asked.

"He'll tell us tomorrow," said the horse, "after he goes to Kindergarten."

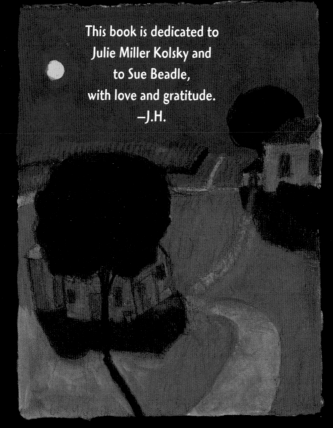

This book is dedicated to
Julie Miller Kolsky and
to Sue Beadle,
with love and gratitude.
—J.H.

G. P. PUTNAM'S SONS A DIVISION OF PENGUIN YOUNG READERS GROUP. PUBLISHED BY THE PENGUIN GROUP. PENGUIN GROUP (USA) INC., 375 HUDSON STREET, NEW YORK, NY 10014, U.S.A. PENGUIN GROUP (CANADA), 90 EGLINTON AVENUE EAST, SUITE 700, TORONTO, ONTARIO, CANADA M4P 2Y3 (A DIVISION OF PEARSON PENGUIN CANADA INC.). PENGUIN BOOKS LTD, 80 STRAND, LONDON WC2R 0RL, ENGLAND. PENGUIN IRELAND, 25 ST. STEPHEN'S GREEN, DUBLIN 2, IRELAND (A DIVISION OF PENGUIN BOOKS LTD.). PENGUIN GROUP (AUSTRALIA), 250 CAMBERWELL ROAD, CAMBERWELL, VICTORIA 3124, AUSTRALIA (A DIVISION OF PEARSON AUSTRALIA GROUP PTY LTD). PENGUIN BOOKS INDIA PVT LTD, 11 COMMUNITY CENTRE, PANCHSHEEL PARK, NEW DELHI - 110 017, INDIA. PENGUIN GROUP (NZ), CNR AIRBORNE AND ROSEDALE ROADS, ALBANY, AUCKLAND 1310, NEW ZEALAND (A DIVISION OF PEARSON NEW ZEALAND LTD). PENGUIN BOOKS (SOUTH AFRICA) (PTY) LTD, 24 STURDEE AVENUE, ROSEBANK, JOHANNESBURG 2196, SOUTH AFRICA. PENGUIN BOOKS LTD, REGISTERED OFFICES: 80 STRAND, LONDON WC2R 0RL, ENGLAND.

PUBLISHED SIMULTANEOUSLY IN CANADA. MANUFACTURED IN CHINA BY SOUTH CHINA PRINTING CO. LTD. DESIGN BY GINA DIMASSI. TEXT SET IN HIGHLANDER BOOK. LIBRARY OF CONGRESS CATALOGING-IN-PUBLICATION DATA HARPER, JESSICA. A PLACE CALLED KINDERGARTEN / JESSICA HARPER ; PICTURES BY G. BRIAN KARAS. P. CM. SUMMARY: WONDERING WHY THEIR FRIEND TOMMY HAS NOT COME TO THE BARN AT HIS USUAL TIME, THE ANIMALS BECOME ALARMED WHEN THE DOG TELLS THEM THAT HE HAS GONE TO A PLACE CALLED "KINDERGARTEN." [1. HUMAN-ANIMAL RELATIONSHIPS—FICTION. 2. DOMESTIC ANIMALS—FICTION. 3. KINDERGARTEN—FICTION. 4. HUMOROUS STORIES.] I. KARAS, G. BRIAN, ILL. II. TITLE. PZ7.H231343PL 2006 [E]—DC22 2005010398

5 7 9 10 8 6 4

SPECIAL MARKETS ISBN 978-0-399-24785-9 NOT FOR RESALE